W9-AHH-363

Little, Brown and Company

Hachette Book Group
1290 Avenue of the Americas, New York, NY 10104
Visit us at lb-kids.com
mylittlepony.com

LB kids is an imprint of Little, Brown and Company.
The LB kids name and logo are trademarks of Hachette Book Group, Inc.

The publisher is not responsible for websites (or their content) that are not owned by the publisher.

First Edition: November 2015

ISBN 978-0-316-41077-9

10 9 8 7 6 5 4 3 2 1

CW

Printed in the United States of America

Licensed By:

THE REASON FOR THE SEASON

Adapted by **Louise Alexander**
Based on the episode "Hearthbreakers" by **Nick Confalone**

LITTLE, BROWN & COMPANY
LB kids

Pinkie Pie and Applejack arrive at Twilight Sparkle's castle just as Spike is putting the finishing touches on some decorations.

The Princess of Friendship smiles. "Happy Hearth's Warming Eve, friends!"

The Earth ponies are so excited! This year, their families will be enjoying the holiday together in Pinkie Pie's hometown of Rockville!

Applejack asks, "What are you and Spike doing to celebrate, Twilight?"

"Since Spike can't sleep unless he opens his presents, we always open them together on Hearth's Warming Eve."

Applejack is surprised. Her family always waits to open presents at the crack of dawn on Hearth's Warming Day. Doesn't everypony?

Soon, Twilight waves good-bye to Pinkie Pie and Applejack, and Spike joyfully starts ripping the wrapping paper off his presents.

As the train to Rockville rushes through the countryside, the ponies fill themselves with holiday cheer. They nibble on frosted snow cones, rock candy stalactites, and more!

Between biles of sweet holiday treats, Apple Bloom exclaims, "Hearth's Warming is the best! I can't wait to open presents!"

"Don't forget the true meaning of Hearth's Warming!" Applejack says. "We celebrate when the Earth pony, Pegasus pony, and Unicorn pony tribes came together to keep the Windigos from freezing the whole world. On Hearth's Warming, we remember it was harmony that brought the pony tribes together to create Equestria. That's why one Apple family tradition is to raise the Equestrian flag!"

"The Pies raise the flag, too!" exclaims Pinkie Pie. "And we eat a big Hearth's Warming Eve dinner to honor friendship between the tribes."

"We have a feast, too!" says Applejack.

"And we hang dolls to remember the warmth our ancestors brought to the world!" continues Pinkie Pie.

"Us too!" replies Applejack.

"And open presents?" asks Apple Bloom.

"Yes." Pinkie Pie laughs. "Of course!"

"And family!" Apple Bloom adds as the train pulls into Rockville. "Being with family is one of the best parts of the holiday!"

"I hope our families like each other," Applejack worries.

"We are best friends, Applejack. And after tonight, our families will be best friends, too!" says Pinkie Pie.

Soon, the group arrives at the Pie family farm, aglow with holiday crystals and minerals.

Pinkie Pie's father lifts a hoof to greet them. "Hello, I am Igneous Rock, and this is my wife, Cloudy Quartz. Thou are most welcome."

Pinkie Pie's sisters—Limestone Pie, Marble Pie, and Maud Pie—nod hello as their mother waves the guests inside.

"Thou must be famished. Enter our home, and we shall begin our Hearth's Warming Eve feast!"

The Apples sit down at the table, surprised. In front of each of them is a giant bowl of soup...with a *rock* in it.

Applejack is confused. *Where are the puffy hot rolls? Is the cider still warming up? Does the potpie need more time to bake?* The Apple family taps at the rocks in their bowls while the Pies eagerly start slurping. Things are tense.

Applejack looks on the bright side. "Isn't it great to have our families together?"

As Applejack starts to realize that their families might not share the same holiday traditions after all, Pinkie Pie declares, "Time to put out our Hearth's Warming dolls!"

The Pies lead the Apples into the rock quarry.

"Uh, do y'all mean these rocks are our Hearth's Warming dolls?"

"Don't be silly." Pinkie Pie laughs. "We *make* our dolls!"

Remembering her soft, crocheted
Hearth's Warming dolls back at Sweet
Apple Acres while she chips away
at a rock, Applejack misses her own
family traditions.

As if reading her mind, Pinkie Pie
calls out over the clanging. "I'm so
happy I get to show you how the Pie
family does Hearth's Warming!"

Applejack tries to act excited as Pinkie Pie describes the next activity: a stone-finding game.

"Teams represent the tribes who united to form Equestria. It's tradition to raise a flag on Hearth's Warming to celebrate, so whoever finds the hidden stone gets to raise our flag!"

This Hearth's Warming is definitely different, Applejack thinks. *But that doesn't mean we can't have a good time…right?*

"Hey, Applejack," Pinkie Pie whispers. "After this, we hide our presents!"

"Hold up, Pinkie Pie. Y'all hide your presents?" Applejack tries to be patient.

"Of course! Although most years nopony finds one." Pinkie Pie looks down with embarrassment.

Applejack yells out, "Lemme get this straight. You eat rocks, you make a doll out of rocks, and then you hunt around for more rocks? And to top it off, you might not even find presents... which would probably be more rocks!"

"Well," Pinkie Pie whispers, "it doesn't sound very fun when you put it *that* way."

Applejack decides it is time to take Hearth's Warming into her own hooves.

"It's not too late to show them the best Hearth's Warming ever," Applejack whispers to her family.

"These are *their* traditions. Try to learn something new and enjoy this time with your friend and her family," scolds Granny Smith.

"Eeyup," echoes Big Mac.

Ignoring their advice, Applejack sneaks out to bring the Apple family traditions to Rockville.

The next morning, everypony is shocked to find the farm decorated with holly, ribbons, and candles. A giant flagpole rises out of the ground, dripping with lights.

"What hast thou done to my farm?" Igneous exclaims.

"Was thou not having a good time?" Cloudy asks, hurt.

Maud Pie points. "Why is there a pole coming out of the fault line?"

Crrrrraaaaacccck.

The ground below the pole splits open, sending beautiful decorations and a pile of presents flying. What a mess!

Looking at everypony's disappointed faces, Applejack feels awful. "I am so sorry, y'all," she cries. "I was so focused on having my version of a perfect holiday that I missed the chance for our families to make new traditions together."

"Well," Pinkie Pie replies, "it's not too late...."

Later that night, the Pie and Apple families decorate the mantel with rock dolls and share a tray of savory hot rolls with apple butter.

"Happy Hearth's Warming to all..." Applejack raises her roll.

"And to all a good night," Pinkie Pie chimes in.

Big Mac nods. "Eeyup."

"Mmm-hmm," Marble Pie agrees.

As everypony warms their tails by the fire, Maud Pie, not the best singer but full of holiday spirit, serenades the group with a song from the Hearth's Warming Day songbook.

"Hearth's Warming Day rocks like gneiss.
And sharing traditions is oh so nice.
Here's to making new friends for life
While we celebrate warming the world from ice."

Even though they might celebrate differently, the ponies know that harmony is the reason for the season.